Meet Wenlock and Mandeville!

Barry Timms

Adapted from **Out of a Rainbow,**
a story by **Michael Morpurgo**

First published by
Carlton Books Limited 2011
Manufactured under license
by Carlton Books Limited
Design and text adaptation copyright
© Carlton Books Limited 2011

London 2012 emblems: ™ & ® The London
Organising Committee of the Olympic Games
and Paralympic Games Ltd (LOCOG) 2007.
London 2012 mascots: ™ & ® LOCOG
2009-2010. All Rights Reserved.

Carlton Books Limited, 20 Mortimer Street,
London, W1T 3JW.

A CIP catalogue record for this book is available from
the British Library.

10 9 8 7 6 5 4 3 2

ISBN: 978-1-84732-495-5

Text adaptation: Barry Timms
Creative direction: Clare Baggaley
Images supplied by: Crystal CG
Production: Kate Pimm
Printed in China

FSC
www.fsc.org
MIX
Paper from
responsible sources
FSC® C101537

CARLTON

This is the story of two very special
creatures called Wenlock and Mandeville.
They came to life in a truly magical way –
and all because of Grandpa George.

It all began when a great rainbow appeared in the sky over the steelworks. Inside, Grandpa George was hard at work, helping to finish a huge girder. It would be used to build the Olympic Stadium, far away in London.

But when the girder was lifted high into the air, a fiery-hot drop of molten metal fell away. It hit the ground with a splosh and broke in two, right by Grandpa George's feet.

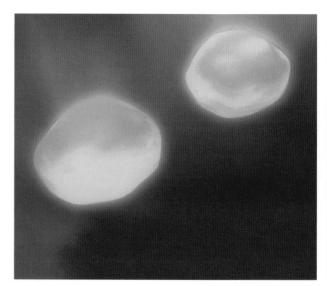

Now, that day was a special one for Grandpa George – his very last day working at the steelworks. How pleased he was to see the girder finished at last!

'Three cheers for George!' called his friends as the working day ended.

It was then that George remembered the two drops of metal on the ground. They were hard now and cool enough to pick up. So he popped them in his bag and waved goodbye to his friends.

Grandpa George cycled home from work
for the very last time. The two special drops of
metal would remind him of all the happy days
he had spent at the steelworks.

Back at home, George's twin grandchildren, Lily and Jack, rushed out to greet him. 'We've got a surprise for you!' they cheered.

George followed them inside, with Unity the dog jumping and barking all the way. And there on the table was a delicious cake! It looked just like the Olympic Stadium.

'Lily and Jack made it all by themselves,' chuckled Grandma, cutting George a large slice.

That night, when all was quiet in the house, Grandpa George was still wide-awake. The two drops of metal in his bag had given him a wonderful idea…

'Shhh,' George whispered to Unity the dog as they tiptoed down the stairs together. They crept through the moonlit garden and into George's workshop.

Soon, strange buzzing and banging noises could be heard in the night air…

Inside the workshop, Grandpa George worked with his tools. Slowly and carefully, he used them to shape the two dark drops of metal. And as he worked, the two shapes became brighter and brighter – until they shone like silver!

Unity sniffed at the metal shapes and wagged his tail in wonder.

When Lily and Jack came down for breakfast in the morning there was a special box for each of them. Grandpa and Grandma lifted the lids and the twins peeked inside.

'Wow!' the children exclaimed when they saw the two shining figures.

'They came from the girder we were making for the Olympic Stadium,' explained Grandpa George. 'They like to be kept shiny and bright – it makes them feel alive.'

Lily and Jack picked up the figures. At once, they felt a magical tingle in their fingers and rushed upstairs to play.

'They will be our special friends,' said Jack as they placed the figures side by side on the sunny windowsill.

Just then, a dark cloud passed over the sun. 'Look, it's raining,' said Lily. 'And there's a rainbow too!' she gasped.

Suddenly the rainbow shone into the bedroom, its colourful rays striking the two figures. As if by magic, the figures started to move – stretching and blinking and looking all around them.

'They're alive!' cheered the twins, clapping their hands with excitement.

And in no time at all, the creatures began to copy everything they saw and heard.

When Lily and Jack giggled, the creatures giggled too.

When Unity barked, they copied the sound and barked back at him.

And when Lily tried a cartwheel, they copied her exactly, learning all the time.

Next, the creatures explored the bedroom. Its walls were covered with pictures of sport and its shelves were full of books about the Olympic and Paralympic Games. Everywhere they looked were athletes – leaping, running, boxing and racing.

The creatures couldn't wait to try these things themselves.

So they leapt ...   and ran ...

and boxed ...

and raced...   There really was no stopping them!

Dr. William Penny Brookes

Much Wenlock

An Inspiration For The Modern
Olympic Games

Just then, one of the creatures spotted a book about a
town called Much Wenlock. This town helped to inspire
the idea for the modern Olympic Games.

The creature had a little think for a moment and decided
to call itself Wenlock.

The other creature found a shining trophy from the Stoke Mandeville Games. This event helped to inspire the idea of the Paralympic Games for people with disabilities. And so the second little creature chose the name Mandeville.

Suddenly the room filled with colours. The rainbow had returned. Wenlock and Mandeville leapt up onto the windowsill, longing to go outside.

'Please don't go so soon!' cried Jack.

'You're our friends – we want you to stay!' said Lily.

But both Lily and Jack knew it was time for their new friends to go off on their travels. The twins thought of all the fun they would have following Wenlock and Mandeville's adventures. They felt sure they would see them again very soon.

So Lily and Jack opened up the window. There in the sky was not one, but two dazzling rainbows!

Wenlock jumped out onto one rainbow and Mandeville jumped onto the other. They couldn't wait to tell people all around the country about the London 2012 Games. And they knew that in 2012, when they finally arrived in London for the Games, the whole world would be watching!

Wenlock and Mandeville turned to wave goodbye to the twins. And then they set off, running up the rainbows and far into the distance.

When Grandpa and Grandma came in to see what all the excitement was about, the two rainbows were still shining in the sky.

'Wenlock and Mandeville went away on the rainbows,' said Jack, a little sadly.

'But we know we'll see them again!' said Lily.

'I do hope so,' said Grandpa George. 'They are the best little creatures I've ever made. There's something very magical about them.'

And far off in the distance, Wenlock and Mandeville sparkled in the sun.

The End

Between now and 2012, Wenlock and Mandeville
will be travelling the UK, meeting new people
and learning all about the Olympic
and Paralympic Sports.

Follow their journey and join in at:
london2012.com/mascots